K! BEEP! BEEP!

BEEP!

BEEP! BEEP!

BEEP!

D1123335

BUSY BUSY →

CITY STREET

by Cari Meister

illustrated by Steven Guarnaccia

Viking

HONK! HONK!

VIKING
Published by the Penguin Group
Penguin Putnam Books for Young Readers, 345 Hudson Street, New York, New York 10014, U.S.A.

Penguin Books Ltd, Registered Offices: Harmondsworth, Middlesex, England

First published in 2000 by Viking, a division of Penguin Putnam Books for Young Readers.

1 3 5 7 9 10 8 6 4 2

LIBRARY OF CONGRESS CATALOGING-IN-PUBLICATION DATA
Meister, Cari.
Busy, busy city street / by Cari Meister; illustrated by Steven Guarnaccia.   p. cm.
Summary: Taxis, trucks, horses, buses and more all hurry along a busy, noisy city street.
ISBN 0-670-88944-X
[1. City and town life Fiction. 2. City traffic Fiction. 3. Stories in rhyme.]
I. Guarnaccia, Steven, ill. II. Title.
PZ8.3.M5514Bu 2000 [E]-dc21 99-42058 CIP

The text is hand lettered
Printed in Hong Kong

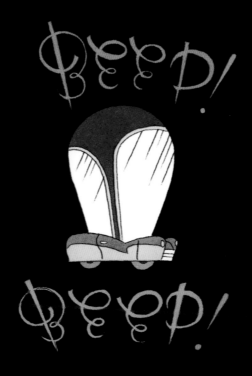

BEEP!

BEEP!

FOR PATTY AND ADRIAN
— C.M.

FOR BERT DODSON AND RANDALL ENOS
— S.G.

HONK HONK BEEP BEEP

Siren sounds, fire call.

Taxi jam, traffic stall.

Busy,
busy
city
street.

Dumpster truck lost
a load.
Garbage mess in
the road.

HONK!

HONK!

B U S Y , B U S Y

BEEP! BEEP!

CITY STREET.

Green light, horses go.

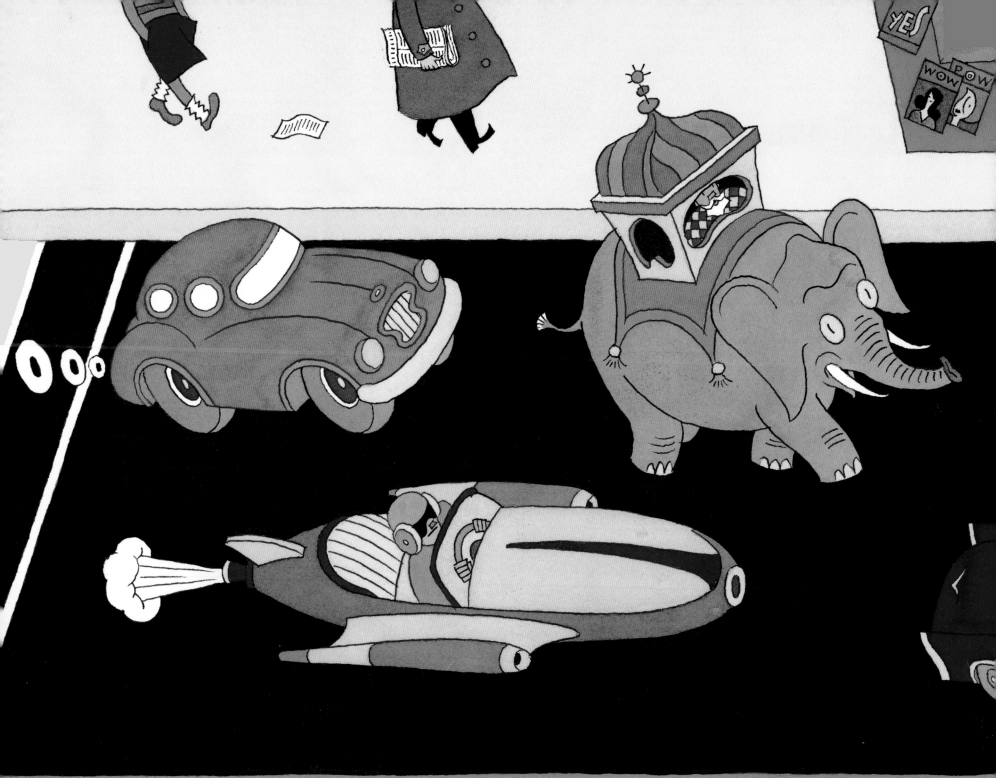

Clippety-clop, steady, whoa!

HONK
HONK
BEEP
BEEP!

Postman, postman in
a flurry.
Postal parcel. Hurry! Hurry!

Heading home,

One by one.

Honk!

HONK!

HON

HONK!

HON

Honk

Honk!